Ship of Ghosts

by

Nigel Hinton

Illustrated by Anthony Lewis

Harper Road
London
SE1 6AF
TEL: 020 7525 9116/0

Globe
Academy

You do not need to read this page -
just get on with the book!

First published 1999 in Great Britain by
Barrington Stoke Ltd
10 Belford Terrace, Edinburgh, EH4 3DQ

This edition published 2001

ISBN 1-84299-002-0
Previously published by Barrington Stoke Ltd under ISBN 1-902260-33-3

Printed by Polestar AUP Aberdeen Ltd

MEET THE AUTHOR - Nigel Hinton

What is your favourite animal?
Beavers
What is your favourite boy's name?
Joey
What is your favourite girl's name?
Sara
What is your favourite food?
Bacon and potato pie
What is your favourite music?
1950s Rock and Roll,
Bob Dylan and Blues
What is your favourite hobby?
Reading

MEET THE ILLUSTRATOR - Anthony Lewis

What is your favourite animal?
Cats
What is your favourite boy's name?
Stephen
What is your favourite girl's name?
Victoria
What is your favourite food?
Yorkshire pudding
What is your favourite music?
Blur and Lyle Lovett
What is your favourite hobby?
Going to the theatre
and travel

For Don and Tor

Contents

This story was inspired by an old
folk song, called WILLIAM GLENN.
I first heard it sung by a great singer
and guitarist called Nic Jones.

"Mick," she called.

I stopped and she ran to me and kissed me and held me tight.

"Take care," she whispered.

I could feel my eyes start to water so I pulled away from her and went out of the door.

A clock was striking four o'clock when I walked up the gangplank of the *Shamrock*. Two hours later we steamed out of the harbour.

As we sailed away from land I saw someone run out onto the harbour wall. It was my mother.

I think she wanted to stop me leaving.

But it was too late.

In the Dark Night

The first night on board the *Shamrock* I was so excited that I found it difficult to sleep. My bunk was in a tiny space next to Captain Glenn's cabin. I lay there listening to the throb of the engine and the creak of the ship as we sailed south.

Then the screaming began.

I sat up in the darkness and listened to that terrifying sound coming from the Captain's cabin. On and on it went. Scream after terrible scream.

Suddenly it stopped.

There was a long moan and the sound of someone sobbing. Then it faded and all I could hear was the throb of the engine and the creak of the ship again.

Captain Glenn

The next day nobody said anything about the screams and I quickly forgot about them as I got caught up with my new life.

The *Shamrock* was only an old cargo ship but to me she was the finest ship on the ocean. The ten sailors on board were a rough lot. They had no uniforms and their clothes were old and oily. They swore at each other all the time and were always ready for a fight. But they were hard workers and I thought they were the best crew in the world.

I was young and my young eyes saw only what they wanted to see.

All I saw was the blue of the sky and the endless waves of the ocean. Each morning I woke to a new adventure. My school friends were still at their desks looking at maps of Africa while I was sailing down the African coast. I was feeling the heat that they could only read about. I was visiting ports that were just names on an atlas for them.

I had never been so happy in my life. The work was hard but I loved it. Every day I polished and scrubbed Captain Glenn's cabin until it was spotless. And every day he noticed and praised me.

"You're the best cabin boy I've ever met," he said one day.

I felt a stupid grin burst on to my face and my heart swelled with pride. All I wanted to do was please him.

I was not the only one. The whole crew liked him. They swore and fought amongst themselves but when the Captain gave them an order they did it at once. And they did it well.

Many of them had been at sea longer than he had but they said he was the best – a born sailor.

They trusted him.

The sea is a dangerous place. And you need to trust your captain because your life is in his hands.

I say that all the crew admired him but there was one man who did not. Yan Chung, the Chinese cook.

The Secret Worlds

Every day, when I finished cleaning Captain Glenn's cabin, I had to help Yan Chung as he cooked in the galley. I peeled and chopped vegetables for the crew's meals and I washed the dishes afterwards.

Yan was small and bent. His face was covered in thin wrinkles and his long, grey hair was tied in a pigtail. He was a wonderful cook and he made some of the best meals I have ever tasted. And he was a great story teller.

He had been at sea for over fifty years and while we worked in the steam and heat of the galley he used to tell me about his life.

"I been ever'where in this world," he said one day when I was washing up. "I seen ever'thing in this world. I know ever'thing in this world. And I know things from the secret worlds, too."

"What secret worlds?" I asked, up to my elbows in greasy water.

"The secret world in here," he said, tapping the side of my head. Then he fixed his black eyes on me and he whispered, "And the other world. The one that live right next to us. But we don't see."

"What do you mean? Ghosts?" I laughed.

"You not laugh," he said sharply, pointing his finger at me. "It is here. All around us. Eyes not see it but it is here. Just ... here."

He held his hand in front of my face and a shiver ran up my back.

He saw me shudder and he nodded, "It is there – you feel it."

Then he smiled and began talking about something completely different. He was like that. One minute he could chill my blood and the next moment he could tell me a story to make me laugh.

It was never dull in the galley and I liked working for Yan. The rest of the crew used to shout at me when I made a mistake, but not Yan.

He only got angry with me once. He was telling me stories about the many captains he had sailed with.

"I bet Captain Glenn is the best," I said.

"You idiot boy. You young."

"Oh come on, Yan. He's got to be the best. The whole crew says so."

"They all idiot, like you. They know nothing."

"Oh yes," I jeered. "We're all wrong. And clever Yan Chung is the only one who's right."

"Yes, I right," he yelled with fury in his eyes. "Yan is right and idiot crew is wrong! Captain Glenn is bad luck man! Is dark cloud round him. He bad luck man. I know. And you know nothing, idiot boy."

Terror in the Sea

I didn't care what Yan said – he was just a strange old man. I liked Captain Glenn. And so did the rest of the crew. And we had good reason.

The voyage was going well and it was all due to our Captain. He had contacts in every port along the west coast of Africa so we never went short of work. We steamed slowly southwards dropping off cargo at one port and picking up a new load to carry to the next.

The weather was fine. The ship was in good shape. And we were all earning extra money from the busy trade we were doing.

Then, one day, a couple of things happened that changed what I felt about Captain Glenn.

The ship was anchored off the coast while we waited for high tide so we could get in to a small port. It was a hot day and a few of us scrambled down a rope for a swim in the warm blue sea. After ten minutes the others climbed out but I decided to stay a bit longer.

I was floating lazily on my back when I heard a sudden shout. I opened my eyes and saw Captain Glenn leaning over the side of the ship. To my horror I saw that he was aiming a rifle at me. There was a bang and a bullet hit the water.

I saw him take aim again.

"No, don't –" I started to shout.

"Get out of there!" he yelled. "Get out now!"

His voice was so fierce that I began swimming in terror. Above the sound of my frantic splashing I heard two more cracks of the rifle.

Then I reached the rope and hauled myself up. I got clear of the water and looked down just in time to see a huge black shape passing below me.

It was a shark.

Its sharp fin cut through a wave then it flicked its tail and disappeared under the ship.

I was so shocked that I could hardly climb the rope. When I got near the top Captain Glenn leaned over and pulled me up to the deck.

"You all right?" he asked.

I nodded and then I started to shake – half from cold and half from fright. The Captain smiled and took off his jacket and put it round me.

"Go on, Captain Mick," he laughed, giving me a salute, "... get below and change into some dry clothes."

My Father

I had just finished dressing when Captain Glenn came down on his way to his cabin.

"I'm afraid it's a bit damp, sir," I said, holding out his jacket.

"It'll dry."

"Thanks for ... what you did just now," I mumbled.

"Well, I couldn't let a shark eat my best sailor, could I?" he chuckled.

Again, I felt that stupid grin on my face. And a blush was creeping up my neck.

"I mean it," he went on. "I've watched you at work. You're going to be a fine sailor. Must be in your blood."

He turned and opened his cabin door.

"It is in my blood," I blurted out.

He looked back at me.

"My Dad ..." I began.

And I told him. I told him everything I knew about James Lane.

"So, he doesn't even know you exist?" he asked when I finished.

"No, sir."

"Oh well, perhaps you'll meet him one day," he said kindly and went into his cabin.

I was just hanging my wet towel over a warm pipe when the door opened again and the Captain looked out.

"Did you say *James* Lane?" he asked.

I nodded.

"Green eyes? Blond hair?"

I nodded.

"Jimmy Lane! I don't believe it! I know him. We were on a cargo ship together in the South China Sea – oh, must be ten years ago."

"What?" I gasped.

"Well, there can't be many blond, green-eyed James Lanes about, can there? It must be him."

"You know him! You know my dad!" I said, my heart beating fast.

"Of course I do! We were on the same ship for nearly two years sailing between Hong Kong and Singapore. And come to think of it ..." he stopped and peered at me. "I knew you reminded me of someone. It's my old friend, Jimmy. You look just like him. Your eyes, the nose ..."

It was too much. I had to turn away to hide the tears.

"That's all right, Mick," the Captain said gently and he put his arm round my shoulder.

"What ... what's he like?" I managed to ask at last.

"Oh, he's a good sailor, Mick. The best. You'd be proud of him. And he'd be proud of you."

I couldn't go on. If I stayed, I would break down. I ran up the stairs out on to the deck.

I stood at the side of the ship and looked out to sea.

My father was a good sailor. The best.

I would be proud of him and he ...

As I said, my feelings towards Captain Glenn changed that day. He had saved my life. And now, to top it all – he knew my father. He was my father's friend.

Before that day, I had liked the Captain. Liked him and admired him. He had been a sort of hero to me. But now it was more.

Now, I was ready to die for him.

Or to kill for him.

A Warning

The next time Yan dared to say anything against Captain Glenn it was my turn to get angry.

We had finally reached the southern tip of Africa. Normally, the *Shamrock* would turn round here and head back north. But the morning after we docked at Cape Town the Captain called a meeting of the crew.

"Listen, lads," he said. "I had a bit of luck today. I met an old friend of mine in port. He's got an urgent cargo bound for Australia and another cargo for us to bring back. I've spoken to the *Shamrock*'s owners in London and they're happy for us to go ahead. It's a long time at sea but the money'll be damn good. It's up to you ..."

Of course, everyone wanted to go. Everyone except Yan. But it was all of us against him, so we went.

We loaded the cargo that afternoon and we steamed out of Cape Town in the evening.

The next day, when we were cooking the meal, Yan started going on about what fools we all were.

"You think only money," Yan grumbled. "You don't see danger. Indian Ocean is big. They big storm there. We just little ship."

"Yeah, but if Captain Glenn thinks we can do it ..." I began.

"I tell you before, idiot boy. Captain Glenn is bad luck man."

"You shut up, Yan!" I shouted, raising my fists. "You say another word about him and I'll ..."

I was only small but Yan was even smaller and he backed away from me, looking scared.

Suddenly I felt ashamed of frightening an old man. I lowered my fists.

"I not say a word," Yan said quietly. Then even more quietly, he added, "You good boy, Mick. That why I warn you. One day you go see I right."

He came back to the table and we got on with our work in silence.

And in the silence, Yan's warning kept going round and round in my mind.

Never Let Go

Yan was right.

The Indian Ocean is big. It is huge. Huge and deep. And the *Shamrock* was a small ship.

You know loneliness when you are over a thousand miles from the nearest land. And you know fear when the water below you is as much as five miles deep. It's best not to think about it.

I did think about it one day.

I was leaning over the edge of the ship, painting the hand rail, when I almost slipped. I grabbed hold of the rail just in time and I pulled myself back on deck. I stood there with my heart pounding with shock. Supposing I had fallen?

How long would I be able to swim before I finally slid below the waves? I imagined myself slowly sinking. Salt water filling my lungs. My body being crushed by the weight of the ocean.

I saw myself floating down and down until I came to rest in the darkness at the bottom. My bones trapped and pressed down by five miles of water above them.

It took us twenty days to cross that ocean and every evening Captain Glenn and I had a chat in his cabin before I went to bed.

The day I nearly fell in, I told him what had happened.

"You know the first rule that sailors have to learn?" he said.

"No, what?"

"Never let go!" he laughed. "Good rule that – never let go!"

I loved those evening talks with Captain Glenn. He told me about his years at sea. The ships he had sailed on. The places he had visited. The people he had met. But what I most wanted to hear about was my father.

"It was a long time ago," he always said.

But I kept nagging him and every day he managed to remember another small detail about James Lane. And, bit by bit, I began to build up a picture of my father.

He was a radio operator. He was really good at his job.

He had a great sense of humour and was always laughing and telling jokes. And he was popular with all the other sailors.

He loved curries.

He was a good swimmer. He had even saved someone from drowning one day.

He'd cut his hand badly once but he didn't have a scar.

He could speak Chinese really well.

They were only small details but Captain Glenn was right. My father sounded like someone I could be proud of. And every night before I went to sleep, I thought about him.

Bad Sign

The day we arrived off the coast of Australia I teased Yan badly.

"Terrible crossing we've had!" I joked. "All those big nasty storms!"

"We still got go back," was all he said.

We landed at Fremantle and unloaded the cargo. Then we had two days' leave while the new cargo was loaded and we took on supplies.

Most of the crew sat in bars getting very drunk. I spent my time walking round the docks.

Maybe James Lane didn't sail between Hong Kong and Singapore anymore. Maybe he sailed round the Australian coast. Maybe he was here. Maybe I would bump into him on the next corner.

I didn't meet him, of course. And after two days on safe, solid land we set off back across the Indian Ocean.

On the second evening out of Fremantle, Yan looked out of the small porthole in the galley and pointed at the sky.

"New moon – she got old moon in her arms."

I looked out to see what he meant. The thin curve of the new moon was shining brightly but the rest of it was almost hidden in the dark.

And it did look a bit as if the new moon was holding the old moon in her arms.

"So what?" I asked.

"It bad sign. It mean bad weather," Yan said. "Bad weather. And bad trouble."

The Trouble Begins

The next morning the sun was shining and the sea was calm.

"Bad storm out there!" I said to Yan as I went into the galley.

He looked away and didn't say a word. I kept teasing him all day long but he said nothing.

Then, in the evening, the trouble began.

I was having my usual chat with Captain Glenn when there was a knock at his cabin door. It was Joe Young, the chief engineer. He was covered in coal dust and oil from the engine room as usual. But he wasn't his normal cheerful self. He looked pale and he was trembling.

"What's up, Joe?" Captain Glenn asked.

"I'm feeling really rough, Skipper. And I'm not the only one. One of my stokers, Eddie Ford, has got it, too. We're puking our guts up. I think we've been poisoned."

"Poisoned?" Captain Glenn shouted. He stood up and his face was twisted with anger. "Don't you dare use that word on my ship."

I'd never seen the Captain lose his temper before. He was always so calm and spoke softly even when he was giving orders.

Joe and I looked at him, shocked by this sudden outburst.

"Sorry, sir," Joe said. "I meant ... you know ... we must've eaten something bad or ..."

Then he swayed and leaned against the door as a wave of pain hit him. His face was chalky white and he was sweating.

"We're going to have to close the engine down, sir. I can't ..."

"That's all right, Joe," the Captain said.

All his anger had gone. He was calm and in control again. He patted Joe on the shoulder.

"You go and lie down. As you say, it's probably something you've eaten. Or you've picked up a bug. A good night's rest and you'll be fine tomorrow. Don't worry about the engine. I'll look after it tonight."

Joe nodded and staggered out of the cabin.

"Come on, Mick," the Captain said. "We've got work to do."

Death comes on Board

The Captain and I worked in the engine room for twenty hours non-stop. One of the stokers, Dave Roach, was there to help us for the first couple of hours. Then he, too, suddenly started being sick and had to go and lie down.

"Ever'body ill, now," Yan said when he brought our breakfast down to us the next morning.

"They all say it my food. But my food good. I tell 'em. Captain not ill. Mick not ill. I not ill. We all eat same food. But they not listen."

"Don't worry about that, Yan," the Captain said. "You keep looking after them. And we'll handle the ship."

All day long the Captain and I shovelled coal and kept the boilers going and the engine running. We were sweating and tired and our hands were covered in blisters but we didn't stop.

Then, in the evening, Yan came down again.

"Joe Young, he puke blood now. He go die, Captain. We got to ask help on radio."

"OK," the Captain said and he went up to the radio room.

I started to shovel coal again but I could feel Yan looking at me.

"What's up with you?" I snapped.

"What Yan tell you?" he said. "Death come on board this ship."

I turned away and forced my aching muscles to go on working.

Half an hour later, the Captain came slowly down the steps. His face was grim.

"Can't get the damn radio to work. It's had it."

Then he looked at both of us and his eyes were dark.

"Joe Young's dead," he said softly.

We tried to go on working but our bodies were too tired and our hearts weren't in it.

"We can't go on like this. We need sleep," the Captain said at last. "Go and get some rest, Mick.

And you, Yan. I'll shut down the engine. The sea's calm enough. We can drift around a while without any danger."

I went upstairs and fell into my bunk.

An hour later, I woke in the darkness and heard screaming. It was coming from the Captain's cabin.

Screams of terror.

They went on and on and on.

From Bad to Worse

The next day, Captain Glenn refused to come out of his cabin.

Every time I knocked on his door he told me to go away. Finally I dared to open the door. He was lying on his bunk.

"What should we do about Joe Young, sir?" I asked.

He said nothing. He just kept staring at me with his sunken eyes.

I went back to Yan and we decided we would have to act without the Captain. The weather was very hot and sticky – we couldn't leave Joe Young's body any longer.

We put a heavy bag of nails on his chest to make sure he would sink. Then we sewed him into a sheet. We carried him to the edge of the deck and laid him on a plank of wood. Then we lifted the plank and let him slide over the side.

Yan chanted some Chinese prayers. I stood there thinking of Joe's long, long journey down to the bottom of the ocean. Then we went back to looking after the rest of the crew.

Dave Roach and the other stoker, Eddie Ford, both died that afternoon. Again, Yan and I sent their bodies sliding down into the dark waters.

Night came but the air got hotter and hotter. There was no breath of wind. And the sea was calmer than I had ever seen it.

It didn't feel right and I began to be afraid.

I was lying on my bunk trying to sleep when the screaming began again.

Without the noise of the ship's engine to cover them, the screams sounded so loud in the night. I didn't want Yan and the others to hear Captain Glenn like that, so I went into his cabin.

Murder

Captain Glenn woke up the moment I opened the door. He sat up quickly, covered in sweat.

"Oh God, help me!" he cried and pointed to the dark corner. "He's there!"

I went over to his bunk and knelt down next to him.

"There's nobody there," I said. "It's just a nightmare."

He shook his head and looked at me. His eyes were filled with terror.

"We're all going to die! He's there, look at him! He came to tell me we're all going to the bottom of the sea with him."

"With who? Who are you talking about?"

"Him!" he pointed into the corner. "Oh thank God! Thank God – he's gone."

Tears filled his eyes and began to slide down his face.

"I killed him, Mick. It was terrible. I poisoned him and watched him die. It took him an hour ... and all the time ... he lay there cursing me."

In spite of the heat, a cold shiver slid down my back.

"Who?" I asked. "Joe Young? The others?"

"No, not them," the Captain sobbed. "It was someone else ... a sailor ... in Hong Kong ... We were in love with the same girl ... and I thought ... if I could get rid of him ... Oh God, I must've been mad ... I gave him poison ... and ... when he was dead, I ... I threw him into the harbour ... Oh Mick, he was my friend."

The Captain suddenly gripped hold of my arm and pulled me towards him.

"He waits until I'm asleep and then his ghost comes to me ... from the sea ... he's covered in slime ... and his eyes ... his eyes have been eaten by fish. And now – it's going to happen to us."

I stood up and pulled my arm out of his grip.

"Don't go!" the Captain cried. "Don't leave me alone. You're my best sailor. My friend."

I opened the cabin door and went out.

And with the Dawn ...

I stood on the deck for the rest of the night, staring at the flat sea. It looked smooth and oily in the moonlight.

Suddenly the stillness was broken by splashing. Hundreds of eels rose to the surface.

They twisted and tangled their bodies together as if they were fighting over something. Their jaws gaped and I could see their sharp teeth. And I wondered if eels ate the eyes of dead men. Then they sank down into the depths again.

But the twisting and tangling went on inside my mind. Captain Glenn was a murderer. But he was my hero. He was a poisoner. But he was my father's friend. He had taken someone's life. But he had saved mine.

I was torn in two.

I stood there and watched the first rays of the sun begin to rise above the horizon.

And with the dawn, out of nowhere, clouds began to block out the light. Huge clouds. Huge and black and boiling. They darkened the sun and began racing towards the ship.

And with them, came the wind.

You could see it swirling across the sea, whipping up the water.

The wind hit me.

One moment the air was warm, the next it was cold.

One moment I could breathe, the next the air was filled with water.

The ship tilted and I fell to the deck. I began crawling. I reached the doorway. I threw myself inside and pushed the metal door closed just as the first wave hit us.

The storm had begun.

The Truth

There was nothing Yan or I could do.

All the men who ran the engine room were dead. The rest of the crew were getting better but they were still too weak to help. All we could do was pray that the *Shamrock* would ride out the storm.

The poor ship did her best. But without her engine, she was at the mercy of the weather.

The wind howled and roared. And the sea shook and battered us. Sometimes we hit the waves just right and went sweeping up to the top before tipping forward and plunging down the other side. But sometimes huge walls of grey water crashed right on top of us and tried to push us under.

All day and all night we stayed in the main cabin. We hardly said a word, just held on tight and listened to the *Shamrock* creak and shudder as she battled the sea.

Then, as the new day dawned, we saw an enormous wave tower above us. It hung for a moment and then came smashing down. It hit us from the side and pushed the *Shamrock* over. We were all flung across the cabin.

For a long time it felt as if the ship would roll right over. We held our breath but then she groaned and, oh so slowly, she swung upright again.

And at that moment I remembered what Captain Glenn's ghost had said – soon we would all be at the bottom of the sea. And, as I thought of the ghost, everything suddenly came together.

A sailor. Hong Kong. My father.

I threw myself to the door and staggered along the passage to Captain Glenn's cabin.

He was still lying on his bunk and I went up to him and grabbed hold of him.

"Was it him?" I screamed into his face. "Was it my father?"

"Mick, we're going to die," he said, and tears filled his eyes.

"Damn you!" I yelled. "You damn coward. Did you kill him? Did you poison James Lane?"

"James Lane?" he said, looking at me as if he didn't know what I was talking about. Then, suddenly, he laughed strangely. "James Lane? You stupid little ... I never met any James Lane. I made him up. You wanted to hear about him so I made him up!"

The Curse of the Murderer

I walked out of the Captain's cabin and I felt all hope drain out of my heart. I was never going to meet my father.

And as the hope drained away, my heart filled up with dark anger.

I hated Captain Glenn.

He had given me a father. He had given me something to dream about. And it was all a lie. It was worse than if he had killed him.

I went back to the main cabin and I stood in the centre of the cabin and the crew looked at me. As the ship rocked and the sea thundered all around us I told them Captain Glenn's secret. And as I told them, I knew what would happen. And I knew who would start it.

And, sure enough, Yan turned to the others as soon as I had finished speaking.

"The curse of the murderer," he said. "That why we have bad luck. He bad luck man. I always know. We all go die if he stay on ship."

There was a long pause.

Then Yan spoke again. "What we go do?"

Man Overboard

We dragged Captain Glenn out of his cabin and up the stairs.

He kicked and screamed and begged us to let him go but our ears were deaf. He tried to hold onto the steps but we stamped on his fingers until he lost his grip.

We pulled him out into the wild storm. The deck was wet and we slipped and stumbled as he struggled to get free. But we slid him closer and closer to the edge.

Then we grabbed his legs and we grabbed his arms and we swung him. Once. Twice. Three times.

And on the third swing we let go and he went flying over the side and down into the raging sea. The waves closed over him.

Then, to our horror, we saw a hand come out of the water. It seized hold of the rope that was trailing down the ship's side. The same rope that I had climbed up when Captain Glenn had saved me from the shark.

Slowly, the Captain began to pull himself out of the water. We watched him haul himself up, hand over hand. Then, as he neared the top, the rest of the crew moved away from the side. I was the only one left.

There was a terrible roar and we both saw the huge wave sweeping towards the ship.

"Mick," he called. "Please help me – you're like a son to me."

He reached a hand up towards me.

"You're not my father," I said.

"Please!" he screamed.

I shook my head.

For a long, long moment he looked straight in my eyes. Then he let go. He broke the rule he had told me about. He let go.

The wave smashed against the ship. Tons of spray hit me and knocked me off my feet.

When I got up and looked over the side, the Captain had gone. He had started his long, slow journey to the bottom of the ocean. Two hours later, the storm died down.

"You see," Yan said. "Bad luck finish now."

The next day, another ship found us drifting on a calm sea. They asked us what had happened to the Captain and we all told the same story: he had been swept overboard by a big wave.

They towed the *Shamrock* back to Australia.

The crew split up and all got work on different ships. None of us wanted to see each other again.

I stayed in Australia and found work on a sheep farm, far from the sea.

I never met my father.

Blood and Dreams

There is blood on my hands.

When I was very young I helped to kill a man.

I am very old now, but I can never forget what I did.

And at night my sleep is filled with terrible dreams.

Dreams of him.

He has been dead many years and his bones lie at the bottom of the sea. But he haunts me still.

Who is Barrington Stoke?

Barrington Stoke was a famous and much-loved story-teller. He travelled from village to village carrying a lantern to light his way. He arrived as it grew dark and when the young boys and girls of the village saw the glow of his lantern, they hurried to the central meeting place. They were full of excitement and expectation, for his stories were always wonderful.

Then Barrington Stoke set down his lantern. In the flickering light the listeners were enthralled by his tales of adventure, horror and mystery. He knew exactly what they liked best and he loved telling a good story. And another. And then another. When the lantern burned low and dawn was nearly breaking, he slipped away. He was gone by morning, only to appear the next day in some other village to tell the next story.

If you loved this story, why don't you read . . .

The House With No Name

by Pippa Goodhart

Can secrets live on after death? Jamie's father buys a house that has been empty for 35 years. A tragic secret from the past is revealed. Only Jamie and his new friend can uncover the full truth. Find out what he discovers in the house with no name.

Visit our website!
www.barrringtonstoke.co.uk